GREAT JOB, DAD!

Holman Wang

tundra

Tundra Books, an imprint of Penguin Random House Canada Young Readers,
a Penguin Random House Company

Library and Archives Canada Cataloguing in Publication

Wang, Holman, author, illustrator
    Great job, Dad! / Holman Wang.

Issued in print and electronic formats.
ISBN 978-0-7352-6410-6 (hardcover).—ISBN 978-0-7352-6411-3 (ebook)

    I. Title.

PS8645.A5318G73 2019   jC813'.6   C2018-900664-1
                                               C2018-900665-X

Published simultaneously in the United States of America by Tundra Books of Northern New York,
an imprint of Penguin Random House Canada Young Readers, a Penguin Random House Company

Library of Congress Control Number: 2018935607

Edited by Samantha Swenson
Designed by Kelly Hill and John Martz

The artwork in this book was created through needle felting (in wool),
scale-model set making and photography.
The text was set in Avenir LT Pro.
Drawing on cover by Celia Wang
Endpaper texture by Pannonia/Getty Images

Printed and bound in China

www.penguinrandomhouse.ca

1 2 3 4 5   23 22 21 20 19

Penguin
Random House
tundra | TUNDRA BOOKS

For Celia and Felix

My dad works as a **manager**
from nine to five each day.

At home, though, he's a **waiter**,
except without the pay.

Quite often he becomes **chauffeur**
to several VIPs.

He acts as an **inspector**, too —

it matters what he sees!

He sometimes has to serve as **judge**
to find who's in the wrong.

Perhaps **computer engineer**

when glitches come along.

By night he's our **librarian**
with stacks of books piled high.

By day he earns his **pilot** wings
and flies us through the sky.

At times he is an **architect**
designing roofs and walls.

And even our **receptionist** —

he has to take our calls!

Let's not forget **astronomer**

who knows the stars above.

Dad does one job to pay the bills,

the others out of love.

BEHIND THE SCENES

with Holman Wang

I think of my illustration process as something akin to moviemaking. First, I cast the characters. In my case, I create 1:6 scale figures in wool through needle felting — a painstaking process of sculpting wool by repeatedly stabbing it with a specialized barbed needle.

Next, I scout locations for outdoor photography, build scale-model sets for indoor shoots and acquire or make all the pint-sized props I need for particular scenes. Then I get behind the camera! After a lot of trial and error, I usually manage to capture an image that's worthy of the final step: a little digital editing in post-production.

Sometimes, my photographs borrow a technique which was common in B movies of the 1950s and 1960s: forced perspective. This is an optical illusion where an object may appear smaller or larger, or nearer or farther away, than it actually is.

By using a short focal length and placing the scale-model sets and wool figures close to the camera, I was able to seamlessly integrate the foreground miniatures in the same photograph with real-life outdoor backdrops and even rooms in my own house. It's not quite Hollywood, but hopefully you'll find a little magic just the same.

Holman Wang is a lawyer who also finds time to make children's books. He and his brother, Jack, are the twin powers behind the board book series Cozy Classics and Star Wars Epic Yarns, which abridge literary and cinematic classics into just twelve words and twelve needle-felted images.

In 2015, Holman and Jack created a Google Doodle celebrating Laura Ingalls Wilder. Their unique artwork has been exhibited around the world, including at The Original Art exhibition in New York (Society of Illustrators), the Bologna Children's Book Fair and the National Museum of Play.

Holman lives with his wife and kids in Vancouver, Canada.

Visit his website at **www.holmanwang.com**